RICHARD WRIGHT and the LIBRARY CARD

by WILLIAM MILLER illustrated by GREGORY CHRISTIE

LEE & LOW BOOKS Inc. • New York

LEE & LOW BOOKS Inc., 95 Madison Avenue, New York, NY 10016
leeandlow.com

Manufactured in China by RR Donnelley

Book Design by Christy Hale
Book Production by The Kids at Our House

The text is set in Congress
The illustrations are rendered in acrylic and colored pencil

(HC) 20 19 18 17 16 15 14 13 12 11
(PB) 35 34 33 32 31 30 29 28 27
First Edition

Library of Congress Cataloging-in-Publication Data
Miller, William.
Richard Wright and the library card/by William Miller; illustrated by Gregory Christie.
p.   cm.
Summary: Based on a scene from Wright's autobiography, *Black Boy,* in which the
seventeen-year-old African-American borrows a white man's library card and devours
every book as a ticket to freedom.
ISBN 978-1-880000-57-1 (hardcover)   ISBN 978-1-880000-88-5 (paperback)
1. Wright, Richard, 1908-1960—Juvenile fiction. 2. Afro-Americans—Juvenile fiction.
[1. Wright, Richard, 1908-1960—Fiction. 2. Afro-Americans—Fiction. 3. Books and
reading—Fiction. 4. Libraries—Fiction.] I. Christie, Gregory, ill. II. Title.
PZ7.M63915Ri 1997
[Fic]—dc21   97-6847   CIP AC

For my son Julian,
books are the road to the promised land—W.M.

To Kim Risko—G.C.

Richard loved the sound of words. He loved the stories his mother told about the farm where she grew up.

"There was a willow tree by a bend in the river," she explained. "I dreamed all my girl dreams down there."

Richard loved to hear his grandfather tell about the war, how he ran away from his master and fought the rebel army.

"I was only a boy," his grandfather said proudly, "but I fought as well as any man. I fought in the rain and the mud. I carried the flag at the head of the troops."

Richard longed to read stories on his own, but his family was very poor. They moved often, looking for work in different towns and cities. His father cleaned office buildings; his mother cooked in the kitchens of wealthy white people.

Richard had little chance to go to school. His mother taught him when she could, reading the funny papers out loud, sounding each word carefully.

When Richard finally learned to read, he couldn't buy or bor-row the books he wanted so badly. Books were expensive; the doors of the library were shut against him because he was black.

So Richard read whatever he could find—old newspapers, books without covers pulled from ash cans....

When Richard was seventeen, he caught a bus to Memphis. He hoped to find work, earn enough money to move to Chicago, where he would make a new life for himself in the north.

Richard walked the hot streets looking for a job that would be his ticket to freedom. He saw many young men, like himself, searching for the same job, the same way out.

He finally found a place in an optician's office. He polished eyeglasses, swept the floors, and ran errands for the white men.

As long as he kept his head down, as long as he began every sentence with "sir," Richard was safe.

At night, Richard returned to the boardinghouse where he had rented a room. To save money, he ate beans from the can, warmed by water from the tap.

Listening to the noise of the street below his window, Richard felt a familiar hunger for words. There were thousands of books in the public library, but only white people could get a card, could take them out.

But Richard had an idea. At work, he looked around the office, trying to find one man who might understand his hunger for books.

For the most part, they were like so many white men he had known before. They would never understand a black boy who wanted a library card, a black boy who wanted to read books even they didn't read.

Only one man seemed different from the others. Jim Falk kept to himself, and the other men ignored him, as they ignored Richard. Several times, Richard had been sent to the library to check out books for him.

One day, when the other men were out to lunch, and Jim was eating alone at his desk, Richard approached him.

"I need your help," Richard said.

"Are you in some kind of trouble?" Jim asked with a suspicious look.

"I want to read books. I want to use the library, but I can't get a card," Richard said, hoping Jim would not laugh in his face.

"What do you want to read?" Jim asked cautiously. "Novels, plays, history?"

Richard felt confused. His mind was racing so fast, he couldn't think of a single book.

Jim said nothing, but reached into his desk and brought up a worn, white card. He handed it to Richard.

"How will you use it?" Jim asked.

"I'll write a note," Richard said, "like the ones you wrote when I got books for you."

"All right," Jim said nervously. "But don't tell anyone else. I don't want to get into trouble."

"No, sir," Richard promised. "I'll be careful."

After work, Richard walked through the crowded streets to the library. He felt as if he were on a train to Chicago, as if he were traveling north already.

But when Richard walked through the door, he felt the old
fear again. Many heads were raised at the sight of a black boy
in the library.

Richard kept his eyes down, not looking up until he stood
before the check-out desk.

The librarian put on her glasses to make sure she wasn't
seeing things. Richard handed her the note he had written
and stepped back.

"Why can't Mr. Falk get his own books?" she asked sharply.

"He's very busy," Richard replied, his legs trembling.

"All right," the woman said. "But you tell Mr. Falk I'd rather
see him in person next time."

Richard roamed the stacks, unable to believe there were this
many books in the world. He touched the leather spines and
fingered the pages he had dreamed about for such a long time.

"Are you sure these books aren't for you?" the librarian asked in a loud voice when he went to check them out.

Once again, heads turned and Richard felt the eyes of white people on him.

He thought he had been caught, that he would never be able to read the books he wanted so badly. But Richard told the lady what she wanted to hear, what she believed was true about all black boys like him.

"No ma'am," he said. "These books aren't for me. Heck, I can't even read."

The librarian laughed out loud and stamped his books. Richard heard other people laugh as he walked out the door.

That night, in his room, Richard read until the sun dimmed the electric light. He read the words of Dickens, Tolstoy, and Stephen Crane. He read about people who had suffered as he had, even though their skin was white. They longed for the same freedom Richard had spent his life trying to find.

With the light of the sun coming through the window, Richard put down the book. He felt sleepy, but the words he had read echoed in his ears, colored everything he saw. He wondered if he would act differently, if others would see how the books had changed him.

Richard knew he would never be the same again.

That morning, he carried his books to work in a newspaper. Whenever he had a chance, whenever the office was empty for a moment, he read.

Mr. Falk walked over, pretending that he was asking Richard to go and pick up his laundry for him. "What'd you get?" he asked under his breath. Richard opened the newspaper and showed him.

Jim seemed shocked at first, but then a smile came over his face. "Those are powerful books Richard," he said. "Those books will stay with you for the rest of your life. But for now," he said, looking around the office, "you should keep them to yourself."

Richard tried to do just that, but as the time for the journey north came closer, he didn't care who saw him reading.

The men in the office either laughed at him or asked him if he was crazy: "What's a colored boy like you toting a bag full of books around for? Your head can't hold all them big words!" Every now and then, Jim smiled at him from across the room.

The library books had changed some of Richard's feelings about white people. Richard still feared them, but he understood them better.

The day he left for Chicago, Richard stopped by Mr. Falk's desk.

"Thank you," Richard said. "Thank you for the books, thank you for everything...." Jim didn't say a word, but he shook Richard's hand in front of everybody.

On the train going north, flying across the open fields, Richard remembered the books he had read.

The words came back to him, the stories more real than the train itself. Every page was a ticket to freedom, to the place where he would always be free.

AUTHOR'S NOTE

Richard Wright and the Library Card is a fictionalized account of an important episode from the life of Richard Wright.

Wright was born on September 4, 1908, near Natchez, Mississippi. His family moved often looking for work, and Richard was educated in a number of different schools. His formal education ended after he completed the ninth grade. In 1926, he moved to Memphis and worked for an optical company. During this time, he gained access to the public library with the help of a co-worker. He read many books during this period which inspired him to become a writer.

Richard moved to Chicago in 1927 and worked for the post office before publishing his first stories. His novel *Native Son*, published in 1940, became an international bestseller. *Black Boy*, his autobiography, was published in 1945 to great acclaim. This book is based on a scene from *Black Boy*.

Richard Wright died in France in 1960.